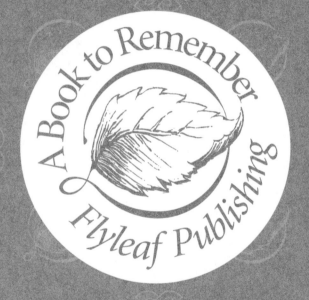

A Book to Remember

Flyleaf Publishing

Shep the Sheep of Caladeen

Written by
Laura Appleton-Smith

Illustrated by
Carol Vredenburgh

Laura Appleton-Smith holds a degree in English from Middlebury College.
Laura is a primary schoolteacher who has combined her talents in creative writing with
her experience in early childhood education to create *Books to Remember*.
She lives in New Hampshire with her husband Terry.

Carol Vredenburgh graduated Summa Cum Laude from Syracuse University and has worked
as an artist and illustrator ever since. Now happily settled in New Hampshire, Carol thoroughly enjoyed
the adventure of illustrating this book and getting to know Shep.

A Book to Remember™
Published by Flyleaf Publishing
Post Office Box 287, Lyme, NH 03768

For orders or information, contact us at **(800) 449-7006**.
Please visit our website at **www.flyleafpublishing.com**

First Edition
Library of Congress Catalog Card Number: 99-90770
Hard cover ISBN 1-929262-01-9
Soft cover ISBN 1-929262-02-7

Chapter 1

The king and queen of Caladeen lived in a castle on top of a hill.

All around the castle was a big green field, and down the steep hill was the deep green sea.

In the field around the castle lived the queen and king's royal sheep.

The sheep were free to eat the royal grass, drink from the royal stream, and sleep on leaf beds under the royal trees.

Each royal sheep had a different name,
and a ribbon of a different color around its neck.

On each ribbon hung a bell with a different ring
so the king and queen could hear the sheep
even if they could not see them.

In the evenings, the king and queen would visit the royal sheep.
They would pat them and feed them from big baskets of royal carrots.

At night, the queen and king
fell asleep to the ringing bells
on their sheep's necks.

You see, the king and queen
of Caladeen had never
had children, so their sheep
were very dear to them.

Chapter 2

The queen and king had a team of royal sheep keepers.

Their job was to keep the sheep clean and trim their fleece when it got long.

Baskets of cut fleece went to royal spinners, weavers, and seamstresses.

Their job was to make the queen beautiful dresses and the king beautiful jackets from the sheep's fleece.

The royal sheep were pleased to see the king and queen
dressed in fabric from their fleece. It made them feel important.

But Shep was different. His fleece was long and had never
been trimmed to make a beautiful dress or jacket.
This made Shep feel sad and unneeded.

Chapter 3

If the queen and king did not need him, Shep felt he must leave. Shep had a plan…

He would sneak from the royal field. He would leap the royal wall and run to the sea. He would see a ship that could take him from Caladeen. His plan was to leave the next night.

On his last day in the field,
Shep nibbled his last nibbles of royal grass.

He drank his last drink from the royal stream.

He peeked at the king and queen in the castle
with a tear on his cheek.

What Shep did not
understand was that
the king and queen
had a plan...

Their plan was
to make Shep's fleece
into the most beautiful
dress and jacket
in all of Caladeen.

Chapter 4

That night, as the queen and king slept, Shep crept from the royal field.

He peeked back at the rest of the sheep. He bleated a soft bleat.

Then he jumped and ran down the steep hill to the sea.

In the castle, the queen was up.

She ran to get the royal trackers.

"Get up, get up," the queen pleaded.

"I cannot hear Shep's bell. He must be lost!"

The royal trackers jumped on their steeds and galloped off into the night.

Half of them went east with the king, and half went west with the queen.

The hill was steeper than Shep had planned.
He slipped on mud and rocks.
Twigs stuck into his soft fleece.

Shep felt weak. Sad and in distress,
he hid next to a big stump and fell asleep.

As the sun crept up past the hill of Caladeen, Shep was not to be seen.

Filled with grief, the queen sat on a stump next to a big rock.

"Where could Shep be?" she asked.

And then there was a soft bleat…

The rock was not a rock, it was Shep!

"Shep, where have you been?" the queen asked as she kissed his soft cheek. Shep bleated a soft bleat of happiness and relief.

Chapter 5

Back in the castle, Shep's fleece was cleaned
and trimmed of twigs and leaves and mud.

Then he was put to bed where he fell into a deep, deep sleep.

When Shep got up, the royal sheep keepers
put a clean ribbon on his neck.

As Shep peeked in the glass,
he could see that his fleece
had been trimmed like the rest of the sheep.

Shep was taken to a feast. All of the sheep and the sheep keepers, the trackers, and the seamstresses, the weavers and the spinners were there.

Shep sat next to the king and queen.

They were dressed in the most fantastic dress and jacket Shep had ever seen.

Shep could see that it was his fleece that made them so beautiful.

It was a grand evening. As Shep fell asleep that night, he had a dream…

It was a dream that the queen and king had hundreds of dresses and jackets made from different sheep's fleece. Each dress and jacket was different, but each one was beautiful just the same.

Shep spent the rest of his days with the king and queen and the royal sheep of Caladeen.

Never again did Shep feel sad or unneeded, and never again did he feel the need to leave.

Shep the Sheep of Caladeen is decodable with the 26 phonetic alphabet sounds plus the "ee", "ea" and "ie" letter combinations. The book also requires the knowledge of the "er", "ed" and silent "e" endings.

Puzzle Words are words used in the story that are either irregular or may have sound/spelling correspondences that the reader may not be familiar with.

The **Puzzle Word Review List** contains Puzzle Words that have been introduced in previous books in the *Books to Remember* Series.

Please Note: If all of the words on this page are pre-taught and the reader knows the 26 phonetic alphabet sounds, plus the phonograms listed above, and has the ability to blend those sounds together, this book is 100% phonetically decodable.

Puzzle Words:

castle
royal
around
even
evenings
children
very
beautiful
important
wall
most
day
again
taken
happiness
color
ship
Shep

Puzzle Word Review List:

the	half
all	or
was	this
down	he
were	she
to	be
so	you
with	I
could	into
would	there
them	put
then	one
than	have
they	of
their	a
night	that
when	where
what	

"ea" words:

eat
east
sea
leaf
hear
dear
team
leap
tear
hear
lead
weak
feast
clean
sneak
bleat
dream
stream
weavers
seamstresses
pleased
pleaded
leave
each
bleated
cleaned

"ee" words:

see
been
deep
feed
feel
keep
need
peeked
seen
free
creep
queen
sleep
steeds
steep
green
trees
asleep
sheep
fleece
unneeded
cheek
Caladeen

"er" words:

ever
under
never
keeper
spinners
weavers
steeper
trackers
different
understand

"ed" words:

lived	jumped
pleased	galloped
trimmed	planned
pleaded	slipped
unneeded	filled
dressed	asked
nibbled	kissed
peeked	cleaned
bleated	

"ie" sound spellings:

field
grief
relief

Silent "e":

make
take
name
made
same
like
nibbles